Scarecrow Slaughter

E.C. HANSON

First paperback edition 2024

 Anuci Press edition 2024

www.anuci-press.com

Cover Design by Chad Lutzke

Home (chadlutzke.com)

ISBN 979-8-9905033-7-3 (paperback)

ISBN 979-8-9905033-8-0(eBook)

For Patrick Moody

Chapter 1

With a torn dress, a busted lip, and dirt in her mouth, Marianne Macdonald limped across a one-way road and crossed onto the Piedmont Farm, a massive property of land that announced its success with a prominent cornfield.

Marianne heard the men's boots behind her, their heavy breathing, too. Two of the mystery men already had their way with her. *What more could they possibly want? Or were there more than two now?*

Marianne rushed toward the cornfield and stopped. *Was there an entrance? Or would she have to make her way through it, hoping that she would lose her attackers and be able to hide until sunrise?*

She heard the men bark orders and realized they intended to split up.

Not good.

Not good at all.

Marianne never saw the men's faces, but she surmised that each of them was twice her size. Energized by cheap whiskey and competing libidos, the men were a real threat to her existence. *Was it because I laughed at one of them? Could I pray to God even though I have never done so before? Will I ever see my sweet husband again?*

Marianne weaved in and out of the cornfield, treating it like a maze. She didn't know which way was right or wrong. All she knew was that the men sounded farther away with each step she took. She grabbed the stout stems of the corn plants and moved through the field, hoping, praying that—

"There she is!" an older man slurred.

Marianne ducked.

All went silent.

Did the man see her?

Marianne crawled aimlessly, swiping at husks, trying to find an exit. She paused. The smell of whiskey. Closer than ever. She curled into a ball and waited.

A full minute passed.

Then another.

The only sound in the night belonged to the screeches of a nearby crow, sitting perched atop an old scarecrow. *Odd. Weren't scarecrows supposed to keep the birds away?*

Another minute passed.

Marianne stood, regained her breath, and chuckled at her good fortune. *The men wouldn't have their way with her after all!*

Marianne studied the scarecrow before her. Its angular and scrunched-up face made it seem like it knew something she didn't. Sharing a similar tone, the crow delivered a single caw.

The harsh sound drowned out the noisy arrival of the men. Marianne turned. While she couldn't make out any of their faces in total darkness, she could tell there were about six or seven of them of varying ages. *All friends? No. All family? Maybe.*

Marianne was cornered. Drunk or not, she couldn't escape this amount of men.

Marianne glanced at the crow again. Instead of belting out another caw, it stared into her soul as if to ask, "Well, are you going to do something before you meet your maker?"

Marianne wrapped her wrinkly hands around the scarecrow and whispered into its straw ear. She rushed through the words because she felt grimy hands on her bony shoulders. It was all about to end for her. She just needed to get a few more words out for the spell to work its magic.

Another set of hands wrapped around her waist. Another set around her throat. Another yanked her ponytail.

Only a few more words and she would get her revenge.

She locked eyes with the crow. Its expression suggested that it didn't think she would be successful. Despite its negative energy, she pressed on.

Chapter 2

Frankie Francona, a rotund and middle-aged gunslinger with rosy cheeks, tilted his plate upside down and allowed the remaining bits of eggs and salt pork to roll onto his waiting tongue. He swallowed, belched, and put the plate back on the table.

"Y'all should ask Frankie if he heard about that."

"If I heard about what?" Frankie asked Joe, the mild-mannered saloon owner.

Joe stepped forward. "About Marianne Macdonald going missing."

"She didn't go missing, you nitwit. She got herself dead," a burly patron said.

"How come?" Frankie asked.

"Piedmonts found her body in the middle of their precious cornfield. Roughed up good, she was. Clothes torn off. Bruises all over her body."

"Now, this here is something I will never understand: men roughing up women," Frankie said.

"How do you know it was *men* that did it?" the patron asked.

"Women don't rough up women."

"So, it's always *our* fault, huh?"

"Yessir."

The burly patron snorted. "You sound like one of them feminists."

"I ain't one of them, and you know it. I do, however, support feminism."

"Then yer a feminist!"

"Oh. Maybe. I don't know what I am." Frankie motioned to the sole bartender in the saloon. "Angie, can you reload my plate?"

Angie raised her eyebrows. "With everything?"

"Everything. Just don't tell my wife."

"Frankie's second plate is coming right up!"

"Ain't you had enough, Frankie?" Joe asked.

"My body tells me when it's enough. My stomach makes a particular sound, and that's when I know to stop, Joe."

"Looks like you shoulda stopped two hundred pounds ago," a gravelly voice in the corner of the room said.

Frankie locked eyes with Jeb Tanner, a full-time pain-in-the-neck who always reeked of tobacco and beer. "Insult me all you like, Jeb. I won't take no offense."

"I've been sitting over here thinking about telling your wife how much you eat, but then again, I think staying quiet is the smarter move. You keep eating, the closer you get to being fit for a casket. If the undertaker's got one big enough for you, Frankie. Heck, not sure there's enough wood in the county."

Frankie slid his chair back and made a move toward Jeb. He leaned over, grabbed him by the collar, and lifted his skinny body out of the booth. Jeb's feet dangled aimlessly, knocking over empty beer bottles. "Make remarks about my appetite, my weight, and whatever else suits you, but keep my wife out of your mouth. Got it?"

"Got it, Frankie. Won't happen again." Jeb said with a smirk.

"I don't believe you," Frankie said as he squeezed harder.

"I got it!" Jeb shouted.

Frankie dropped Jeb on the table; the sarcastic gunslinger fell backward into the booth. Angie brought Frankie another plate of hot food.

"For me?"

"Ain't that what you wanted?" Angie asked.

"I had biscuits on my first plate."

"Then we will get you a biscuit."

"Make it two. Just don't tell my wife," Frankie said with a wink.

Frankie sat at his table and worked his way through a second breakfast. He reflected for a moment about his wife, Shannon. He considered the thought of anyone harming her in the manner that they harmed Marianne Macdonald. He couldn't hold onto the idea for long because it was too much to bear, but he did take a moment to briefly pray for the authorities to find the men responsible for ending Marianne's life. If they didn't, he knew he would become involved. Whether the love of his life approved or not.

Chapter 3

Mikey Piedmont, the youngest son in the family, ventured through the vast cornfield pretending he was in pursuit of an unwanted critter. This was a lie created so he could delay the list of chores his demanding mother had waiting for him. He always wondered why a ten-year-old would have so many chores. He drove the thought from his mind as he forged ahead and slapped the cornstalks without much regard for their value. He hummed a tune. He thought of a joke his friend Sally told him. *What do cowboys call midnight? High moon.* He chuckled long and hard about that one. "Can't wait to tell Pa." Suddenly, he stopped in his tracks.

About fifty feet away, a tired and battered scarecrow swayed in the breeze. Mikey hated the darn things. He always had. But he was more concerned about the object's presence in relation to the date. "Aw, hell. Bad luck's coming our way. Oh yes, it surely is!" A well-known superstition claimed that your family would experience a series of bad luck if a scarecrow remained on your property past November first.

It was the second of the month.

Mikey rushed through the cornfield toward his home but tripped over a broken stalk and fell flat on his face. He looked up at all the cornstalks and felt like they were smothering him, suffocating him. *Was he imagining this?*

Mikey stood, brushed the dirt off his shirt, and turned back to give the scarecrow one more look.

It wasn't there.

Feeling like his eyes deceived him, Mikey walked to where it was not two minutes ago. No scarecrow. No sign of one ever being there, either.

He shook his head in disbelief. The blue sky started to turn dark, which caused Mikey to panic. *Why had he come out here this late? All to avoid his dang chores?*

He inched his way forward, grabbing cornstalks as he went. Then he heard it.

A whisper.

Hoarse yet high-pitched.

He listened. The voice said, "You're first." A maniacal laugh followed.

He stepped forward. Nothing.

Then, the cornstalks began shaking uncontrollably. Violently. Mikey screamed and froze in place. He didn't know where to turn. He didn't know how to get anyone's attention, either. *Could any of his family members hear him scream from a few hundred yards away while these cornstalks rattled so?* Doubtful.

Mikey closed his eyes, worked up a few ounces of courage, and took another step forward. The cornstalks stopped shaking in an instant. Relief washed over Mikey's face. He chuckled.

All became calm and quiet again. He thought of that silly joke he would tell Pa the second he got home.

But when he took another step, the scarecrow returned, and not only was it standing in front of him, but it was now five times its original size.

Chapter 4

The remaining members of the Piedmont family, save the patriarch and matriarch, entered the saloon with a level of force that caused all the patrons to jump out of their seats.

Jack Piedmont, the eldest son in the family, pointed at Joe. His lean frame and clean-shaven face betrayed how intense he could be. "Our precious Mikey's been killed, and we think them whores had something to do with it!"

Offended by his words, Eleanor Dupree, the head of the brothel madams, descended the ornate stairwell like a famous actress summoned to the stage for a big performance. "Lord knows I sympathize with a child being killed. Even if it's a member of your despicable family, Jack. But I hate to break it to you: We had nothing to do with it."

Richard Piedmont, the middle son, intervened. Unlike Jack, his broad frame and severe face announced the evil that lived in his core. He approached Eleanor with his hand cocked back. "Maybe we can slap some sense into ya, and then the truth'll fall outta that skimpy dress."

"The dress isn't skimpy, and I've already told you the truth. Why don't you get Deputy Millburn to investigate?"

"That old rooster?! It's a dang miracle he wakes in the morning after all the booze he consumes. Let's cut the bull, okay?" Richard leaned forward so his nose was pressing against Eleanor's. "Where was ya between the hours of four and six this evening?"

"We've been here."

"Being whores?"

"Keep calling us that word, and we will never help you on this matter," Eleanor said.

Richard hopped behind the bar, cracked a bottle of whiskey, and lit a match. "What do you say, Joe? Want your saloon to go up in smoke?"

"I didn't do anything!" Joe pleaded.

Jack pointed to the madams. "But they did. And they work for you, so we'll call you guilty by that whatchamacallit... association."

"Don't burn my business down. I've had it for thirty years!"

"Well, then, you better help us get some answers. Because all of them girls have had it out for our Pa since God knows when."

"Why don't you hire someone to investigate?" Eleanor asked.

"Who could we hire?" Jack said.

"Money's an issue, fellas?" Eleanor mocked. "I thought after stealing everyone's land in the county and making that unnecessary cornfield, you would never have money troubles again."

"Money isn't a goddang issue. Know what's an issue? Your haggard face." Richard said.

Eleanor chuckled. "I'm impressed by your insults, but we must prepare for the evening. Lots of clients and all. Nice and respectful ones, unlike you."

Jack and Richard stared at Eleanor and the other madams with disdain. Jack grabbed the saloon owner by the wrist. "You got somebody in mind that we can hire?"

"I'll tell you once yer brother stops lighting matches," Joe said.

Richard blew out the matches he was holding behind the bar. "Who besides Deputy Rooster will help us get justice for our little brother?"

"Frankie Francona."

"*He's* a gunslinger?" Jack asked.

Richard guffawed. "More like a foodslinger. Heard he eats everything he comes across."

"That he does, but he only accepts jobs that revolve around two things: injured women or injured children," Joe said.

The Piedmont brothers perked up at the reveal. But before they could respond, a voice from the corner booth caught their attention. "Why would you go and waste your money on that out-of-shape food addict when you got the best and cheapest gunslinger right here?"

Jack and Richard turned to find a slightly intoxicated Jeb Tanner. He stood, pretended the alcohol hadn't impacted his physical and mental state, and stepped forward with his hand held out. "I'll start working right now. Pay me after the job's done." Thinking that their silence was good for his chances, Jeb continued. "We got ourselves one 'a them deals or what? Yeah? Huh? Do we?"

Chapter 5

Jeb stumbled his way through the cornfield, snickering as he went. He used his Remington pistol to smack cornstalks out of his face. He thought about getting justice for the Piedmont boy. He thought about the hefty payday he would receive from the boy's family. And he most certainly thought about using his newfound riches to try and lure Shannon away from that fat blowhard Frankie Francona.

Jeb burped and sniffed the air; the whiskey smell was a comfort in the darkening night. He snapped out of it and focused on his goal. If he solved this matter before the evening concluded, he could hit the saloon and order the most expensive meal and whiskey on the menu.

He searched for clues on the ground.

Nothing.

He searched for clues on each and every cornstalk.

Nothing.

Who would kill a boy of ten years? Could them whores have something to do with it? Nah. No woman is killing a child, regardless of how much of a pain in the behind they are. It just isn't in their makeup.

Jeb heard a rustle. He turned.

Nothing there.

It had to be the wind.

The sound occurred again. This time, it sounded closer. Jeb acted like he wouldn't turn to check, thinking something might be behind him. He took one step forward and spun with his Remington held out.

Nothing there.

Was his mind tricking him? Was the wind doing it? Or was someone out here with him?

"I ain't the kinda feller one plays games with!"

No response.

A powerful breeze rattled the cornstalks and blew off Jeb's hat. He bent to pick it up, but it was dragged across the dirt.

"Don't make no sense," Jeb said, referencing how the hat appeared to be tugged by an unseen force. He approached the hat, bent down, and reached for it. Something yanked the hat away from him again.

It must be the wind. There ain't no other explanation!

Jeb waited for the next round of wind to pass and then dove on top of his hat. "Got it!" He chuckled as he stood and placed the hat atop his head. He glanced at the dark sky and full moon. Unfortunately, his investigation would have to continue the next day.

Jeb got his bearings by locating the farmhouse approximately two hundred yards north. So, that's the direction he started going.

But then his hat blew off.

That was definitely not the wind.

He returned to retrieve his hat.

"Who goes there?"

Jeb walked a few more feet and looked left. Nothing. He looked right and spotted something odd. It was a tall scarecrow on a wooden cross with its arms outstretched. His hat was at the human-like effigy's feet. Scarecrows didn't bother him, but this particular one got under his skin. A stay-away energy was palpable in the air. *And it was just a hat, but it was his hat!* Gifted to him by his father more than thirty years ago.

He took a step forward with his pistol ready.

He estimated that he could snag his hat in six more steps.

One.

He eyed the scarecrow.

Two.

He took a deep breath.

Three, four.

He rubbed the sweat from his forehead.

Five.

He cocked the hammer on his pistol.

Six.

He reached for his hat.

Suddenly, the hat spun in circles and flew on top of the scarecrow's head.

"What and the—"

The scarecrow removed its straw head, revealing a withered and decrepit wolf skull. Jeb screamed at the top of his lungs. But no one in the Piedmont family heard him. They were too far away to know they would soon need to hire another gunslinger.

Chapter 6

Before Frankie dismounted his American Saddlebred, he smelled the food cooking inside his log shack. Despite consuming two plates at Joe's Saloon earlier in the day, he knew—despite the occasional rumbling from his stomach—that he could polish off a full plate of supper and a side of dessert. But the second he entered his home; Shannon was on him like white on rice.

"Y'get anything from the General Store or saloon?"

"Nothing at all. I was good today, Shan."

"Have a seat. Supper's about ready."

Thrilled that he got past her brief interrogation, Frankie tucked a napkin into his shirt collar and grabbed a knife and fork. That's when his stomach betrayed him and rumbled. Again.

Shannon froze at the stove. She shook her head. She turned with a bowl of chicken soup and placed it at her spot. She sat across from Frankie and began eating. Confused on how to proceed, he asked, "Do you want me to serve myself or something?"

"You ain't eating nothing, Frankie. That rumbling in your belly tells me you've already had too much food today, so what was it? Soda pop and candy from the General Store, or a plate with all the fixings at the saloon?"

Frankie sighed. "The saloon. And it was two plates, Shan. Forgive me."

"Forgive you? I oughta whip you good."

"I'm sorry, Shan! I got to talking about this Marianne Macdonald murder, and the food was coming my way. It was either stop the food coming or stop getting information about the woman. It was out of my control."

"What happened to Marianne?"

Before Frankie could provide an answer, he heard the sound of horses arriving on his property. Two male voices rapidly approached the front door, and without knocking, Jack and Richard Piedmont burst into the room.

"Jeb Tanner was murdered!"

"On our property!"

"Because you didn't accept the job!"

"'Cause you were too busy eating candy at the General Store!"

Frankie raised his hand in quick protest. "I was never offered no job, fellas."

"But were you at the General Store today?" Shannon felt the need to ask.

"I may have stopped in there, Shan. But just for a—"

Shannon vacated the table. She couldn't hide her disappointment with her husband. "Would you men like some soup? Calm yourselves down, catch a breath, talk it out slowly?"

"Um, no," Jack said.

"Why would we want *that* peasant food?" Richard asked.

"Why don't we speak outside?" Frankie suggested.

Shannon crossed the room and blocked the front door. "They don't need to eat my soup. But they do need to explain why they interrupted our supper."

"Well, yer the only one eating, Shan, so technically—"

"Fellas, if y'ain't staying for the food, get to the point," Shannon said.

"We want Frankie," Jack said.

"We need Frankie," Richard added.

"Because of what happened to Marianne Macdonald?" Frankie asked.

An awkward silence filled the room as the brothers eyeballed one another. Fighting back tears, Jack spoke first. "Our little brother was murdered."

Shannon covered her mouth with a nearby napkin. "Oh, my!"

"So, with all due respect to Marianne, finding whoever slaughtered our little brother takes precedence over finding out what happened to her."

"The whore," Richard added.

"Should one refer to Marianne as that?" Shannon asked.

"I can," Richard said.

"Well, I can't. There was no proof."

"Whore or not, she was crazy. Thinking she could tell people's fortunes, curse them and whatnot."

"It seems to me that she would be useful to you now. Considering what happened to your youngest."

"That's an argument for another day, Ma'am."

"You coming?" Jack asked.

"Who, me?" Frankie asked.

"Well, we ain't hiring yer dang wife," Richard said.

"How much for the gig? How much do we take in if I find the person or persons responsible?"

Richard Piedmont scanned the interior and snorted. "Enough to leave this sorry excuse of a house."

Jack quickly tried to make amends for his insensitive brother. "I don't know where you got the chicken and vegetables for that soup, Ma'am, but you would have enough money to eat fancy dinners for the rest of your days."

Insulted by their insinuation that she cared solely about money and status, Shannon approached the men with a confidence that intimidated them. "My husband cares more about the victims than his profits."

"Well, then, it's a perfect scenario. Frankie, when can you start?" Jack asked.

Richard placed his hand on Frankie's shoulder. "Tonight?"

Frankie glanced at Shannon. Then, the pot of soup. Then Shannon. Then, the pot of soup. Then, the two brothers.

Shannon approached the stove and loaded up a bowl of soup. "He will start after he's had a home-cooked meal."

"So, what's that mean? Right after he eats or in the morning?" Richard asked.

"At sunrise. Now leave us be, or the deal is off."

The Piedmont brothers exited in a huff.

Once it was evident that the men were officially gone, Frankie dared to speak. "What gives? Why are you giving me soup, Shan?"

Shannon returned to the table, clenched her hands in a quiet prayer, and locked eyes with her husband. "Because someone who kills the likes of Jeb Tanner is a downright awful and dangerous person."

"But you're okay with me messing with it?"

"You have to, Frankie. You have to get justice."

"That don't answer why you gave me the soup?"

"Because it could be your last meal."

"Shan!"

"It could!"

"Do you want it to be my last meal?!"

"No!"

"Sure sounded like it!" Frankie shouted as he marched away from the table.

"Where are you going? You haven't touched your soup yet!"

"For the first time in my life, Shan, I ain't hungry."

Frankie exited his home, feeling guilty for raising his voice at Shannon. But there was no turning back. He didn't know what to do other than the one thing he was customarily paid to do: investigate the crime.

Chapter 7

It wasn't like Frankie to quarrel with his wife, but the mere mention of Jeb Tanner always got his blood boiling. But Jeb was no longer. Therefore, Frankie could focus on two areas: keeping his bride happy and solving the jobs the county hired him for. The present job? Figure out why a cornfield became the site for multiple murders.

Frankie moved through the endless rows of cornstalks with a small lantern to guide him. Standing at six foot four inches, he was impressed that the height of the stalks cleared him by at least a foot.

A caw sounded nearby.

Did that mean the crow saw something?

Frankie always felt like crows could see things he couldn't.

Two more caws.

Determined to locate the crow responsible for the harsh cries, Frankie shifted course. Instead of going up and down the rows of cornstalks, he went side to side, feeling like he would stumble upon what he wanted faster than the alternative. And sure enough, he was right!

But he wished he hadn't been because of the ominous scarecrow that stood before him with a pitch-black crow on its right shoulder.

He also wished he apologized to Shannon. He wished he had eaten the chicken soup. He wished he had snuggled in bed with the woman he had married many moons ago while overlooking a breathtaking mountaintop.

The scarecrow emitted strange sounds and a sinister energy that unnerved Frankie so horribly that he backpedaled and lost his balance; he considered running away like a coward, but he thought that might have an adverse effect on the situation.

"I mean you no harm. I just...I'm trying to get justice for a deceased woman."

The scarecrow leaned back and provided a moment for Frankie to escape. He rushed through the cornstalks, thanking the scarecrow profusely for allowing him to survive.

Frankie had to speak with the Piedmonts about the murders and get more details before he continued. Although he would keep it to himself, one thing he was convinced of was that this scarecrow had something to do with the recent crimes. He didn't understand how that was possible, but he knew it. He felt it tingling in his bones.

Chapter 8

Well aware that the food before him was influenced by the Vaqueros, Frankie Francona couldn't help but ask the Piedmont family—the remaining members (father, mother, eldest son, and middle son) what he was about to consume.

"'S called Son of a Bitch stew," Jack said.

"'Cause a Son of a Gun stew already exists," Richard added.

Frankie couldn't help but chuckle at the hostile and impatient energy emanating from the wealthy family that hired him, specifically from the silent patriarch and matriarch. Their harsh glares seemed to increase the temperature in the room. Knowing he couldn't wait to reveal his findings until after supper, Frankie opted to converse with the sons between spoonfuls of this exotic stew. He ignored the rumbling of his stomach, which told him earlier he should stop eating before he had an accident in his pants or, as Shannon always feared, strained his overworked heart.

"Would one of ya mind telling me what happened to Miss Macdonald?"

"I don't like that question," Jack said.

Richard nodded. "Me neither."

"How would we know what happened to *that* woman?" Jack asked.

Frankie slurped his stew. "Forgive me for asking, but everything started once she was, um, found deceased on the property, right?"

"That's correct," Jack said.

"What are you implying?" Richard asked.

"Boy, oh boy, this stew sure is good."

"Prolly better than that cheap crap your wife makes," Richard said.

Frankie tensed up. "Leave my wife out of this, or you'll see a side of me that'll shock you."

Motivated by his mother's death glare, Jack tried to get back on topic as he paced around the kitchen. "What does that woman dying got to do with what happened to our Mikey?"

"Nothing. Maybe something. I don't got the answer yet. But I will. I always find the answer," Frankie boasted.

"Like the food always finds your mouth?" Richard asked.

"Precisely. Even though my belly is telling me to stop."

"Then stop," Jack said.

"It'd be rude not to finish."

"It'd be rude to accuse us of knowing something when you know nothing," Richard said.

"I did no accusing. But it is a curious situation. Who buried Marianne Macdonald?"

"How would we know? We wasn't part of that kook's family," Richard said.

"Y'all sure got strong feelings about her," Frankie said before he went in for another scoop of stew.

Jack glanced at his mother. Richard looked to his father. The tension mounted. The matriarch finally resorted to words to sell a point.

"We don't know nothing, Mr. Francona. We don't know who raped and murdered Marianne Macdonald." Frankie kept his eyes glued to the remaining stew in his bowl as she continued. "And we don't know what tore our Mikey apart. Nor do we know what got Jeb Tanner. Hell, we wouldn't be seeking your services if we could wrap our heads around what and the heck was happening in our precious cornfield. We'd handle it ourselves if we wasn't—"

"Scared?"

"We ain't scared, Mr. Francona," Mrs. Piedmont said.

"We're not?" Jack asked.

"We ain't," Richard said.

"If we ain't scared, then we don't need him," Jack said.

Mrs. Piedmont motioned to Frankie. "Then fire him."

"I won't take offense," Frankie said as he licked both sides of his spoon.

"FIND OUT WHAT HAPPENED SO WE CAN GO BACK TO LIVING OUR LIVES!" Richard screamed as he chucked a rock-hard biscuit against the wall; a framed photo of the family shattered and dropped to the floor. No one moved. No one said a word.

A slurping sound caused everyone to relax. Frankie finished his bowl, wiped his wet lips with the back of his hand, and burped.

"I have a lead, but I sure am reluctant to share it with ya."

Richard dragged a stool across the floor and sat inches away from Frankie. "SPIT. IT. OUT."

"This, and I must confess that I do not believe in tall tales, might be the work of none other than that enormous scarecrow in the middle of your cornfield," Frankie said.

Laughter. Tons of it. And long-lasting.

Uncomfortable with the family's harsh tones, Frankie waited for the laughter to cease. Even though another morsel of food would make him pop, he couldn't help but notice a fresh lemon pie near the stove. His favorite flavor. Shannon's least favorite. Translation: He never got to eat it unless it was listed on the menu at Joe's Saloon.

"Please tell us you're joking," Jack said.

Frankie's eyes drifted to the stove. "I'll say I'm joking for a sliver of that-there pie."

"He's serious," Richard said.

Jack shook his head. "No, he's not."

Richard sprung off his stool. "Yes, he is. He believes a dang scarecrow did this. I can tell by the look in his eyes."

"If it wasn't a scarecrow, who was it?" Frankie asked.

"Something human. Something...female," Richard said in a daze.

"What does that mean?"

Richard bolted for the back door and exited. After the door slammed, Jack picked up the overturned stool and sat near Frankie. "You was joking, right? Please say you was."

"I was."

Frankie wasn't, but he told Jack this to prevent any more hysteria from blossoming.

"You had us good. Thank the Lord Almighty. For a second, I done believed ya. But there ain't no way this is the work of a scarecrow."

"No, there ain't."

"You're staying the night," Jack said.

"If it's okay with Shannon, I don't see why—"

Mrs. Piedmont intervened. "That wasn't a question, Mr. Francona. You're staying the night, or you don't get paid. Ever."

Jack vacated his stool, grabbed the lemon pie, and shoved it in front of Frankie. "Eat this while I get a room ready for you. The only problem is...our bed situation."

"Ain't gotta bed?" Frankie asked.

"Not one you'll fit in. Might have to shove two or three together."

Unaffected by the insults about his size, Frankie said, "If that's what it takes."

Mrs. Piedmont hovered near the refrigerator. "That boy was our pride and joy. We expect more progress tomorrow."

"You'll have it, Ma'am." Frankie's attention shifted to the silent father. "He talk?"

"Only when it's necessary," Mrs. Piedmont said.

After Jack vacated the room, Frankie felt put on the spot around the intense parents. Not knowing what to say to them, he studied the lemon pie from all angles before committing to his first bite.

Chapter 9

Lying across two beds and still hanging partially over, Frankie snored relentlessly. The lack of comfort never bothered him; he could sleep anywhere.

Suddenly, the door to the guest room burst open. Jack and Richard Piedmont screamed in unison. "THERE'S SOMETHING IN THE CORNFIELD!"

Frankie fell out of bed, rolled over, and stood as if he hadn't been drooling seconds earlier. "What do you see?"

"A lantern. Somebody's crossing through," Jack said.

"And we never permitted nobody to cross through there except you and...Jeb," Richard said.

"Let's go check things out."

Jack sat on the edge of the bed. "We ain't checking nothing out. You're doing all the checking."

"On accounta us paying you and all," Richard said.

Frankie offered up a reminder. "Haven't been compensated yet."

"Y'got yerself a serving of stew, pie, and a pair of beds that barely hold you. I'd say you've been compensated quite nicely so far. The actual money part will come once you solve this case."

"On my way," Frankie said as he fixed his pants, shirt, and jacket. He struggled mightily to slip his black leather boots on.

"Don'tcha think you need bigger boots?" Richard asked.

"Only boots I got," Frankie said in a matter-of-fact manner.

Frustrated that they had to wait longer, Jack and Richard watched Frankie force his boots onto his wide feet. He was out of breath and needed a moment to get his bearings.

Unable to hide his impatience, Richard yelled, "By the time y'get out there, whoever it is could be gone!"

"They could be gone, but they might not be," Frankie said with a confident wink.

Less than ten minutes later, Frankie walked through the cornfield with his lantern (provided by the Piedmonts). He didn't like being here for multiple reasons: he didn't like cornfields, he didn't like investigating at night, he didn't like scarecrows or birds or bugs, and he didn't like anything that fell under the mysterious category. And this investigation, thus far, landed there.

Not fifteen yards before him, he spotted an overturned lantern. Miraculously, the flame remained constant without threatening the valuable crops. Frankie didn't know why the holder would abandon it, but he did know it probably wasn't due to a positive reason. He bent to pick up the lantern and turned to his right. He saw the boots sticking out from between the corn first. He knew he was looking at an older man's body, but he needed to get closer to deduce what happened to the evening visitor.

There were no marks on Sheriff Millburn's body. No signs of a struggle. The only noticeable aspects about his lifelessness were that his eyes remained wide open—as if something petrified him—and a bottle of empty whisky dangled out of his mouth.

Frankie's brain flooded with questions about the sheriff. *Why had he come here?* Known as a dipsomaniac, the sheriff bided his time in jail, avoiding his responsibilities as a protector of the law. So, what prompted the appearance?

Since Frankie couldn't drag the sheriff's hefty body to the Piedmont house alone, he was unsure how to proceed. He pried the bottle out of the man's mouth, thinking it might make the sheriff more comfortable, even though he was already deceased. Little did Frankie know his act would lead to important information, but it did. Hanging off the neck of the bottle was a pink ribbon. It didn't look like something that would be wrapped around a whisky bottle; it looked like a woman's hair ribbon.

Chapter 10

The minute Frankie showed the Piedmont brothers the pink ribbon, he regretted it. Jack stared at it but remained standing in place; Richard, on the other hand, plucked it out of Frankie's grasp and stormed out the back door.

"Where do you suppose he's headed?" Frankie asked, not really wanting an answer.

"You don't want to know," Jack said.

***

Richard Piedmont flung open the doors to Joe's Saloon with the pink ribbon wrapped around his fingers. He noticed a group of brothel madams mingling at the top of the stairwell. "You did this!" Richard shouted as he ascended the stairs. His primary focus was on none other than Eleanor Dupree, who didn't seem to have a care in the world. "This here was found on Sheriff Millburn's body. You madams all got one 'a these dangling from your hair. So please explain to me how it ended up in our cornfield. You explain it to me in one second, or else yer all gonna catch a beating the likes of which you wouldn't even find in your dang nightmares!"

Composed as ever, Eleanor Dupree stared into Richard's soul. "You can yell at us. You can threaten us. You can beat us. But two things will still be true."

"What's that?" Richard asked.

"One: We had nothing to do with what happened to your little brother. And two: You will remain less than a man."

Before a silence settled in, Richard launched the full weight of his body toward Eleanor. Even though he was outnumbered—five to one—he swung his arms and fists around without a care in the world for where they would land. He was only seeking justice for his little brother.

***

When Richard returned to his home, Jack immediately noticed his amused yet maniacal expression and Frankie noticed the blood streaked on his fingers.

"What did you do?" Jack asked.

"Nothing."

"Had to do something to cause that," Frankie said as he pointed to Richard's fingers.

"It ain't my blood," Richard snorted.

"Then whose is it?" Jack asked.

Richard picked up the half-eaten lemon pie on the stove and dug into the dish with his bare hands. He stuffed piles of mushy pie into his mouth and laughed his head off. "Let's just say the blood belongs to various women."

The color drained out of Frankie's face. He wanted to beat Richard until he stopped laughing. Instead, he showed himself the door. "Gentleman, it seems the time for me on this particular job has run out. I do not and will not support violence toward any woman in any way. Thank you and good evening."

Frankie slipped out the back door. Jack slapped the back of Richard's head. After he finished his pie, Richard sprung out of his chair.

***

"Wait up!" Richard shouted.

But Frankie didn't wait. He pressed on at a speed that asked a lot of his spherical body. He didn't want to associate with the Piedmonts, specifically Richard, ever again. Usually at least one of the members of a victim's family would treat Frankie with respect and allow him to conduct his investigation peacefully. The Piedmonts, however, were a different story.

"I'll pay you double to stay on!"

"You haven't paid me nothing yet," Frankie said.

Richard whipped out a stack of bills. "Triple!"

Frankie stopped, turned, and grabbed Richard by the collar of his shirt. "You kill any of them? Any of the women dead from all your nonsensical punches?"

"Naw, no. Not that I know. Eleanor Dupree took the brunt of it, and as far as I know, she was breathing sorta normally when I left. All her whores were tending to her, so she was fine. She's gonna be fine."

Frankie wasn't hearing any of it; he committed to finding his way through the cornfield and out toward the direction of his home.

"Now you listen to me, you fat waste of space." Frankie turned again. Richard's insult didn't amuse him. "I took care of them girls. Spooked them good. This is when you swoop in, talk to all them individually, and force out a confession."

"I don't force women to do anything, Richie."

"But one of 'em killed my little brother!"

"So you say," Frankie said as he assessed how to escape the cornfield.

"If it wasn't one of them, then who was it? Who would do such a nasty thing to a little boy? Huh? Tell me, fatso. Tell me!" Richard shoved Frankie to the ground. Before Frankie could retaliate, the cornstalks swayed aggressively.

Frankie had a clue as to what it foretold; Richard assumed it was a random bout of heavy wind. Moving slowly but surely, the scarecrow crawled behind Richard without him noticing.

"You might want to turn around," Frankie said. Despite not wanting to help this horrible man, Frankie knew Richard's life was in peril.

"And why would I do that?"

"Fair point. Maybe you shouldn't."

Like a child unable to help himself, Richard turned to find the scarecrow rising to the heavens. Its black, oval eyes were as dark as the bottom of the ocean, and its round head showcased a wide mouth filled with sharp, angular teeth.

"Gimme yer pistol, Frankie!"

Even though Frankie tried to assist, the scarecrow didn't give him time to do so. It lowered its long hand under Richard's pant leg, shot upward toward his waist, and ripped his penis clean off his body. Richard screamed, begging for the scarecrow to stop. But the scarecrow sliced both of his arms off next, spun around, and then slit his throat. Blood spurt everywhere as the crop protector approached a gobsmacked Frankie.

Frankie shimmied backward and tried to stand, but the scarecrow hovered above him. He drew his pistol, but it fell out of his sweaty hands. There was nowhere to turn. There was nothing to grab onto, nothing to use as a makeshift weapon. He dug his fingers into the muddy ground and crawled toward his pistol. But the scarecrow knocked it a few yards away from his reach.

Frankie was trapped and moments away from certain death. He thought of how he left matters with Shannon and how he would perish without serving her a proper apology.

But much to his surprise, the scarecrow didn't attack him. It backed away and motioned toward the cornfield's entrance. *Was it letting Frankie go? Or was he being directed there for a particular reason?*

Frankie picked up his pistol, tucked it into his holster, and approached the nearby entranceway. Suddenly, the pitch-black sky turned hot pink, the stars beamed bright, and the wind shifted to whip around the area. *What was Frankie watching? A dream? A new reality?*

Seconds later, Marianne Macdonald, the woman whose death set all these events in motion, ran away from an unseen group. Like Frankie a few moments ago, she was cornered and didn't stand a chance.

Frankie had never had a vision before, so he didn't think his brain conjured this up. It was a "watch what really transpired" presentation by the death-dealing scarecrow. Frankie wanted to remain in good graces with the presenter, so he allowed the scene to play out. And as the attackers stepped into the light, a face appeared.

Then another.

And another.

And another.

And another.

And another.

The scarecrow locked eyes with Frankie. Unmanned with the vocabulary to convey his level of compassion for the horrors that Marianne Macdonald had experienced, he simply covered his mouth.

Chapter 11

Frankie lingered in the doorway of his home while Shannon worked at the stove. He dragged the tip of his boot against the frayed floorboards and waited to receive her full attention.

But she kept cooking with her back turned.

"Sure smells good."

Frankie watched Shannon's shoulders drop as she delivered a note-worthy sigh. He was in the doghouse and needed to find a way out.

"Whatcha making?" Frankie asked.

Finally, Shannon turned with a stirring spoon and pointed at him. "Apologize and I'll tell you. Apologize twice, and I'll serve you."

Apologize twice? Should he say the word sorry twice, or did she mean he had two things to apologize for? He guessed it was the latter.

"I'm sorry for getting upset with you for caring about my well-being, and I am also sorry for..."

Frankie had to think about this one. *What else was there?* He took his mind off the savory smells that shot up his nostrils and closed his eyes.

"...getting upset by you mentioning Jeb Tanner. It's just...he's always had his heart set on you, and I didn't like hearing his name leaving your lips."

Shannon processed both apologies. While she knew she could make Frankie suffer a bit longer, her smirk hinted that she missed his company.

"Have a seat. The food's almost ready."

"It's like you knew I was on my way home!"

"It's always good to be prepared."

"What do you have for us this evening?"

"Salted sowbelly."

Frankie raised his eyebrows.

"Whistle-berries."

Frankie licked his lips.

"And...sourdough rolls."

Frankie glanced at the ceiling and said, "Hallelujah!"

"Watch your volume."

"The closest neighbor is miles away!"

"Still."

"Yes, Shan."

Shannon served Frankie his plate and then made one for herself. She joined him at the table. "You can start."

"Oh, thank heavens."

Frankie wolfed down his meal with the excitement of a young child; Shannon worked her way through her meal methodically as if she intended to relish and remember each bite.

"Any progress with Marianne's case?" Shannon asked.

"Some. A little, yeah."

"Why hasn't there been more?"

"For starters, we no longer have a sheriff," Frankie said as he placed the lawman's badge on the table. "And I get the feeling that there was more than one party responsible for her demise."

"No woman deserves that fate."

"No person does."

"You have to help her, Frankie. Avenge her. For all women."

"Don't I know it."

Frankie wasn't getting the hint. Shannon pressed forward with a new tactic.

"Remember when you fought off five gunslingers who made rude comments about me at the saloon?"

"I sure do."

"Remember when that land baron threatened to take this house, and me, away from you?"

"Remember that, too."

Shannon cocked her head to the side, letting a heavy silence fill the room. A look of understanding crossed Frankie's face. "After supper, you must go back and conclude your investigation."

"Without dessert?"

"I didn't make a dessert."

Frankie dropped his fork and stared at her. It was a first in their marriage. "I don't know what to say."

"That's fine. But you do know what to do." Shannon crossed the table, grabbed the sheriff's badge, and pinned it to Frankie's chest.

"I ain't no lawman. I'm a bounty hunter, Shan."

"You're both for this job."

"How come?"

Shannon pecked him on the cheek. "Because I said so."

"And I gotta do everything you say?"

As she returned to her seat, Shannon said, "Precisely."

Chapter 12

Jack Piedmont answered the front door to find Frankie Francona, filled up on supper, waiting on his doorstep. "Who died and made you sheriff?"

"The sheriff."

"Need to come in?"

Frankie turned and motioned to the cornfield. "Naw, I was hoping you'd follow me through there."

"Why?" Jack asked, but his shaking leg hinted that he was scared to do what Frankie requested.

Frankie tapped his holsters. "Don't you worry. I got my pistols to protect us."

"You'll protect me in case something...happens?"

"Sure will. 'S what I'm being paid for, right?"

"Right," Jack said as he pulled the front door shut.

"Lead the way?"

"You can."

"You can pay me to do so," Frankie said.

Once Jack withdrew a few bills from his pocket, Frankie started walking.

As they reached the entrance to the cornfield, Jack, not one to show much emotion, remained frozen in place.

"Everything okay?" Frankie asked.

"Yeah, yeah. Fine. Just in and out, then?"

"In and out. Say, why don't we talk about something specific to calm your nerves?"

"I don't need to calm my nerves."

"Okay. Whatever you say. We could talk about any number of topics. Marriage, family, weather, or my absolute favorite: food."

"Whatever you like."

"Forget the topics I mentioned. Let's talk about the wild vision I had."

Frankie led the way through the first row of the corn maze, honestly hoping that he would secure a confession from Jack about his involvement in the rape and murder of Marianne Macdonald before the scarecrow made an appearance.

"You ever have visions?" Jack shook his head. Frankie kept talking. "Don't matter if you do. I ain't never had visions, either. Not until yesterday. Want to know where that very vision occurred?"

"Not really."

"Good, so I'll tell you. Walk a few feet that a way."

"Which way? To the left or right?"

"Left. No, right. Wait." Confused, Frankie approached Jack and stood next to him. "Yeah, it's your left."

Jack walked over to where he was told. He stood and waited. Frankie backed away, trying to locate the exact spot where he had the vision. "Close enough. So, here I was walking through this ominous corn maze when, out of nowhere, I happened to see the sky changing colors."

"Why did it do that?" Jack asked.

"So I could see what happened to Marianne Macdonald."

"And did you?"

"Think it's time you owned your part in it," Frankie said.

"I had no part in it."

"Your family did."

Cowering, Jack said, "Okay, but not with me present."

"You were present, Jack. I need you to own your part in order to keep you safe. I can't promise that if you don't come clean."

"What do you need to keep me safe from?"

Frankie turned and studied the cornstalks. They oscillated slowly, providing a much-needed breeze. But Frankie knew that wasn't their intent. The purpose of their movement was to inform Frankie that trouble was on the horizon.

"Feel wind anywhere else, or is it just centered around the cornstalks?"

"I don't know!"

"It's only here. In this area."

"Can we leave?"

"Admit your part in it, Jack. Admit your role in what happened to Marianne."

As Jack tried to form words to sell his repentance, the tall and menacing scarecrow appeared behind Frankie. The thin creature hissed, which caused Frankie to lock eyes with Jack. "If you don't admit to what you did, it will do to you what it did to your brothers. Would you like that?" But Jack was too petrified to answer. "Do you want to get ripped apart?"

"It's..."

"Growing, I know. It can make itself bigger. Own the crime, and maybe it'll refrain from harming you."

"I didn't harm Marianne. But I watched it! I watched Richard and Sheriff Rooster and my father take part. Drunk on whiskey, I just watched!"

Jack burst into tears; Frankie nodded as if the guilty man's words would prevent the possibility of more violence. But the scarecrow rose with its arms outstretched. "I don't think it's gonna give us a hug."

"Then what do we do?" Jack asked.

"You, run, Jack. You run as fast as you damn can!"

Instead of running toward his family's house, Jack bolted into the middle of the corn maze, assuming that the scarecrow couldn't track him.

He was dead wrong.

As Jack frantically pressed through the cornstalks, the scarecrow hovered above him in flight, eager to make its move.

Knowing Jack Piedmont wasn't long for this earth, Frankie shouted some advice. "Apologize for what you did, Jack! You owned your part, but I think you must apologize for it, too!"

Jack paused, switched directions, and aimed his sprint toward his family home. He replied to Frankie's suggestion. "Apologize to a scarecrow?!"

"I know how it sounds! But I think it's the only way or else it will—"

"Or else it will what?" Jack yelled.

Frankie dropped his jaw at the sight of the scarecrow's next move. It stretched a pink ribbon, turned it into a lasso, and flung it around Jack's waist. He kept running forward, but the ribbon became taut and ripped his body in half!

Frankie turned away, unable to watch any further. He slumped to the ground and played with the wet grass. His mind drifted to the comforts of sowbelly, whistle-berries, chili, sausages, jerky, sourdough biscuits, lemon pie, and just about any stew.

Then, he thought about Shannon. And how good he had it. He was lucky to have such a strong and caring woman at home waiting for him. God, he loved her. Even more than the food.

Well, maybe more than the food.

Frankie glanced at the scarecrow as it consumed Jack Piedmont's body. He adjusted his attention to the Piedmont home. From this distance, it looked picturesque. Like the American dream home. But two guilty persons remained inside that home and while Frankie didn't seek more violence, he was committed to delivering justice. As temporary sheriff, he could enter the house and drag the patriarch and matriarch of the ill-reputed Piedmont clan to the county jail. *But would they go willingly? Or would he have to rely on the vengeful scarecrow for assistance?*

Only time would tell.

Chapter 13

While the tension in the kitchen was palpable the second Frankie invited himself inside, the smell wafting from the stove allowed him to break the ice. "Is that a pecan pie?"

"It ain't for you," Mrs. Piedmont said as she lit a cigarette.

"Then who's it for?"

"Not you."

"Well, here's the thing: I ain't accustomed to taking pies that ain't mine; however, the matter of compensation has become dicey based on the facts mined from my investigation. See here, the thing is... How can I accept money from criminals? How could I sleep at night knowing I accepted money from a clan that watched and partook in the heinous killing of Marianne Macdonald? How would I look my wife in the eyes? The truth of the matter is I couldn't. Therefore, I am taking this pie that ain't meant for me, and I am gonna eat the whole dang thing in one sitting while both of you confess to your part in the crime. If you don't, I will escort you to the county jail where your fate will be decided in the coming days once a new sheriff is appointed. *If one is appointed.*" Frankie lowered his nose, so it was inches above the glistening pie and took a big whiff. He smiled as he brought the dish with him to the table and sat in the only vacant chair. "In case it wasn't obvious, this is when you talk."

Mr. Piedmont looked to his wife for how to proceed.

Enraged that this heavyset gunslinger boldly suggested how they should respond to his accusation, Mrs. Piedmont circled the substantial kitchen like a lion ready to pounce on her vulnerable prey.

"You think you're pretty smart, huh?"

"Would never label myself as such," Frankie said.

"But you would accuse us of being involved in Marianne Macdonald's murder?"

"I would do that, yes."

"You would even go so far as to appoint yourself sheriff in your quest to solve what happened to her?"

"Temporary sheriff, but yes."

"Let's say for the sake of argument that we had something to do with Marianne's murder..."

Mr. Piedmont shifted in his seat, causing the chair to make an obscene sound. Mrs. Piedmont rolled her eyes and continued. "...and let's also say that you had concrete proof of our involvement..."

In between stuffing his mouth with pecan pie, Frankie said, "Okay."

"How and the hell would *you* escort us to the county jail?"

"I'd ask you nicely."

"And when that failed?"

"I'd try by force."

"And when I threatened you with this?" Mrs. Piedmont removed a rifle from the wall and aimed it at Frankie's chest. He stopped chewing his pie and wondered if he could draw his pistol and shoot before she did. But he couldn't harm a woman, not under any circumstances, no matter how much she may deserve it. *But what would he do if she fired?*

He turned his attention to the supposedly submissive Mr. Piedmont and realized that the patriarch had a pistol aimed at him, too.

Frankie was trapped. If he shot one of them, he would open the door for the other to end his life. He had never been this close to death. So, he stood, pushed in his chair, and mumbled a "thank you" for the pie as he exited the back door.

He allowed the Piedmonts to get a temporary win. He pondered his options as he stepped off the porch with his hands raised. He bumped into a clothesline and got an idea.

Who could Frankie rely on to make the Piedmonts pay for their crimes? He remembered it wasn't whom he could rely on, but what.

Chapter 14

Frankie knew the likelihood of luring the Piedmonts out to their prodigious cornfield was next to nil. *But the possibility of leading the scarecrow inside their home?* It seemed possible, especially with the help of the parents' clothes. Moments earlier, Frankie had nabbed two items off the clothesline: a gingham dress and a pair of wool trousers.

Frankie walked casually through the maze, taking in the manicured cornstalks. He held up the dress and trousers and shook them as he went. *Was this a stupid idea?* Perhaps. But he had to try.

Then he heard a caw.

And another one.

And another one.

He spun in circles, searching for the crow responsible for putting up such a vocal fuss.

Twenty yards to the west, the scarecrow appeared with its trusty crow perched on its straw shoulders. While it didn't seem to be a threat to him, Frankie wouldn't describe the creature's expression as welcoming. Therefore, Frankie showed off the items he stole from the clothesline. Much to his relief, the scarecrow, filled with rage and its quest for justice, followed Frankie in one direction: toward the wraparound porch of the Piedmont house.

Frankie walked up the porch steps, trying not to make a sound. But his weight was a liability, so he knew that a creak or two might happen. The back door to the home was wide open, creating the possibility for the scarecrow to enter.

Unsure that the creature would understand his directive, Frankie motioned toward the home's interior. He followed it up with, "Go on in. That's where the guilty ones are. Head in and get your revenge."

The scarecrow launched its arm toward Frankie's neck and lifted him. It was no easy feat to lift a man of Frankie's size. *Was the scarecrow going to strangle him? Did it assume Frankie was creating a trap?* Sensing it was the latter, Frankie mustered up a few words despite his airflow being impacted by the creature's firm grip around his throat. "I'm...trying...to...help...you."

The scarecrow dropped Frankie on the porch. *So much for being quiet!* His body sent a reverberating sound throughout the interior of the Piedmont home. But before either parent came to check on what caused it, the scarecrow decreased its mammoth size so it could slip indoors, delivering an excited hiss.

Frankie regained his composure on the porch while he allowed the scarecrow to finish its quest. He heard the patriarch shout curse words, followed by a random gunshot.

There was a heavy silence.

Then, the marching of feet within the home.

A woman's feet. The matriarch's.

Frankie closed his eyes and formed a picture to match what he heard inside the home. Mrs. Piedmont cocked her rifle. She ordered the scarecrow out of her house. She repeated her order.

Another heavy silence.

Then, Mrs. Piedmont screamed, "You killed my boys! You killed my babies!"

Then, a smashed plate.

Then, a gunshot.

Then, a hiss.

Then, a tossed chair.

Then, another gunshot.

Then, a blood-curdling cry from the matriarch.

Then, a heavy thud on the floor.

Frankie turned to see the decapitated head of Mrs. Piedmont rolling in his direction. He dove out of the way. It bounced off each porch step and landed in the tall grass.

Moments later, the scarecrow appeared in the doorway. It lingered there for a minute before it turned into a ghost-like figure of the woman who set this revenge plot in motion: Marianne Macdonald. Frankie studied her, wondering if he should say or do something. He waited her out. In the subtlest way to reveal that she was grateful for his services, she smirked.

Chapter 15

Frankie smelled the calf fries the second he arrived on the property. Shannon never bought or made them because they were considered a delicacy and weren't always available. He heard a rumor that the fries were an aphrodisiac, but Frankie knew that the reason his wife was cooking the dish had to do with the other rumor: they were high in protein and good for your health. *And boy, was Shannon concerned about his health!*

Frankie entered his home, fully expecting Shannon to rush over, hug him, and kiss him on the mouth. But she did none of those things. She was too busy making a dipping sauce for the calf fries.

Frankie slumped in his chair and waited for Shannon to speak. She turned with a hot plate of calf fries and placed them in front of him.

"Eat up. Don't let them get cold."

"Ain't hungry."

"Calf fries are your favorite."

"Ain't hungry."

"Frankie Felix Francona…"

"Sometimes you feel like eating, sometimes you don't."

"What'll it take for you to eat?"

"Nothing."

"You eat those, or, with God as my witness, I will toss them out in the dirt." As Frankie hesitated, Shannon grabbed his plate and marched to the open front door.

"Don't!"

"Why?"

"You gonna eat them?"

"I will so long as you have some."

"I will."

Shannon handed him the plate. She joined Frankie at the table and sensed how different he seemed.

After an extended silence, Frankie asked, "Why do men hurt women?"

"Wish I knew."

"I just do not understand it. No, I do not."

"Me neither."

"In case you was wondering, it's over."

"Over over?"

"It is. The things I seen and heard you wouldn't believe."

"That so?"

"It is. But I won't bore you with it."

"Try boring me with it."

"You believe in curses?"

"No."

"You believe in spells?"

"No."

"You believe in killer scarecrows?"

"No."

"You believe in the human race?"

"No."

"Then what and the heck do you believe in?"

"*You.*"

"Me? Why?"

"Because you're a good one."

"A good what?"

Frankie gnawed on a calf fry as he waited for Shannon to respond. But she never did. She just sized him up with a warm smile, knowing that he was a rare soul and that she should relish every second of his existence.

* * *

About the Author

E. C. Hanson is the author of WICKED BLOOD, MOTHMAN HAZE, and LONE WOLF. He earned his MFA in Dramatic Writing from NYU and was the recipient of an "Outstanding Writing For The Screen" certificate.

He lives with his family in Salem, Massachusetts.